BASKETBALL'S GREATEST STARS

STEPHEN CURRY

by Dave Campbell

SportsZone
An Imprint of Abdo Publishing
abdopublishing.com

abdopublishing.com

Published by Abdo Publishing, a division of ABDO, PO Box 398166, Minneapolis, Minnesota 55439.

Printed in the United States of America, North Mankato, Minnesota
092016
012017

THIS BOOK CONTAINS
RECYCLED MATERIALS

Cover Photos: Marcio Jose Sanchez/AP Images, foreground; Ben Margot/AP Images, background
Interior Photos: Marcio Jose Sanchez/AP Images, 1 (foreground), 24-25; Ben Margot/AP Images, 1 (background), 4-5, 16; Tony Dejak/AP Images, 6; Paul Sancya/AP Images, 7; Seth Poppel/Yearbook Library, 8; Fred Jewell/AP Images, 9; Mary Ann Chastain/AP Images, 10-11; Brett Flashnick/AP Images, 12; Chuck Burton/AP Images, 13; Paul Sakuma/AP Images, 14-15; Jae C. Hong/AP Images, 17; John Bazemore/AP Images, 18; Frank Franklin II/AP Images, 19; Torrey Purvey/Icon Sportswire/AP Images, 20-21; Sue Ogrocki/AP Images, 22-23; Jeff Chiu/AP Images, 26, 27; Eric Risberg/AP Images, 28-29

Editor: Todd Kortemeier
Series Designer: Laura Polzin

Publisher's Cataloging-in-Publication Data
Names: Campbell, Dave, author.
Title: Stephen Curry / by Dave Campbell.
Description: Minneapolis, MN : Abdo Publishing, 2017. | Series: Basketball's greatest stars | Includes index.
Identifiers: LCCN 2016945482 | ISBN 9781680785432 (lib. bdg.) | ISBN 9781680798067 (ebook)
Subjects: LCSH: Curry, Stephen, 1988- --Juvenile literature. | Basketball players--United States--Biography--Juvenile literature.
Classification: DDC 796.323 [B]--dc23
LC record available at http://lccn.loc.gov/2016945482

CONTENTS

TAKING THE TITLE

The last seconds ticked off the clock in Cleveland on June 16, 2015. Golden State's 40-year wait between championships had ended with a 105-97 victory.

Stephen Curry and his teammates started the party. They were finally bringing a National Basketball Association (NBA) title back to Oakland, California.

FAST FACT

Almost 13 years before Curry was born, the Golden State Warriors beat the Washington Bullets for the title with a four-game sweep in 1975.

Stephen Curry, *center*, and the Warriors won Game 5 in front of a wild home crowd to set up a chance to win it all in Cleveland.

Even in defeat, Cavaliers leader LeBron James came over to shake Curry's hand. Netting 13 of his 25 points in the fourth quarter, Curry gave Golden State a big final boost. He added eight assists, six rebounds, and three steals that night.

The Warriors won the series in six games. A few weeks earlier, Curry was named Most Valuable Player (MVP). The sharp-shooting point guard nicknamed "Baby-Faced Assassin" and simply "Steph" was now also an NBA champion.

Curry hit only three of 11 three-pointers in Game 6, but was able to score in other ways.

Curry holds the Larry O'Brien Trophy as a first-time NBA champion.

FAST FACT

Curry won the NBA's MVP award in consecutive seasons, 2014-15 and 2015-16. The second one was by the first unanimous vote in league history.

GROWING UP WITH THE GAME

Stephen Curry had an early start on basketball as a kid in North Carolina. His father, Dell, played 16 seasons in the NBA, mostly with the Charlotte Hornets.

Stephen saw the league up close by tagging along to the arena. He developed many of his skills by playing against his dad in their backyard.

Stephen, *right*, grew up in a basketball family with his father Dell, *top*, in the NBA.

Dell Curry, *30*, played in more than 1,000 NBA games.

Coming out of Charlotte Christian High School, Curry was considered too small by major college basketball programs. He stood 6-foot-1 (1.9 meters) and weighed 160 pounds (72.6 kilograms). Virginia Tech, where his father played, only wanted him as a non-scholarship player.

Instead, Curry chose Davidson College, where he became known for more than just having a famous father.

Curry broke the Davidson College scoring record for a freshman and led them to the NCAA Tournament.

FAST FACT

Curry's mother's name is Sonya. He has a sister, Sydel, and a brother, Seth. Curry and his wife Ayesha have two children, Riley and Ryan.

Curry led Davidson to the 2008 NCAA regional finals as a sophomore. His Wildcats lost by just two points to the University of Kansas, the eventual national champion. As a junior, Curry led the country with an average of 28.6 points per game.

Curry left Davidson after his junior year as the school's all-time leading scorer.

FAST FACT

Curry's younger brother, Seth, is an NBA player himself. He spent the 2015-16 season with the Sacramento Kings. He played college basketball at Duke University.

Curry scored 30 points in the second half against Gonzaga in Davidson's first-round upset in the 2008 NCAA Tournament.

THE SPLASH BROTHERS

Curry left Davidson a year early for the NBA Draft. He promised to return one day and finish his degree. Now 6-foot-3 (1.9 m) and 181 pounds (82.1 kg), Curry was still a little small to be an NBA player.

The Warriors were confident in Curry. They used the seventh overall pick on him. Their faith was rewarded when Curry was runner-up for the Rookie of the Year Award.

FAST FACT

Ankle injuries have been one of the biggest challenges in Curry's career. They began in college and followed him to the NBA. He missed 40 games in the 2011-12 season due to ankle surgery.

Curry holds up his new jersey alongside his parents after being drafted by the Warriors in 2009.

No NBA star can carry a team all by himself. Help arrived in 2011 when the Warriors drafted Klay Thompson. In their second year together, Curry and Thompson led the Warriors to a 47-35 record and a playoff appearance. Over the previous 18 seasons, the Warriors had only qualified once.

The duo became known as the "Splash Brothers," named for their ability to make the ball swish through the basket.

The Splash Brothers of Klay Thompson, *right*, and Curry have been two of the NBA's best shooters since 2011.

Curry won the 2011 All-Star Weekend Skills Challenge that tests passing, shooting, and ball-handling.

FAST FACT

The "Splash Brothers" nickname was a reference to baseball stars Jose Canseco and Mark McGwire of the Oakland A's. They were called the "Bash Brothers" for their home run hitting in the late 1980s.

THE RECORD SETTER

Curry led the league in steals and free-throw percentage in the 2014-15 and 2015-16 seasons. His biggest claim to fame, though, is three-point shooting.

With an effortless motion and near-perfect form, Curry can make a shot from almost anywhere on the court. In 2012-13 he set the all-time record with 272 three-pointers.

Curry collects one of a season-high five steals on January 3, 2014.

Curry won the NBA's Three-Point Contest in 2015.

After leading the league again in 2013-14, Curry managed to top himself in threes. He beat his own record with 286 in 2014-15. Then came the 2015-16 season. He blew the record out of the water, finishing with 402.

Curry was simply dominant beyond the arc on February 27, 2016 in Oklahoma City. The Warriors and Thunder were tied late in overtime.

FAST FACT

Curry has three of the top four three-point season totals in NBA history. Klay Thompson has the other, with 276 made in 2015-16.

Curry steals the ball from the Thunder's Russell Westbrook in their game on February 27, 2016.

With the clock about to run out, Curry pulled up from just a few steps beyond the half-court line. For such a long and tough shot, he took it calmly. It rattled in off the back of the rim. The Warriors won 121-118.

Curry finished with 46 points. He tied the NBA single-game record with 12 three-pointers. He also broke his own single-season mark in the game. After the season, Curry was again named MVP. He received every single vote.

Curry celebrates hitting the game-winner in overtime against the Thunder.

FAST FACT

The three-point line is set 23 feet, 9 inches (7.2 m) from the basket, except in the corners. There, it is 22 feet (6.7 m) away.

BESTING THE BULLS

As defending champions, the Warriors usually faced their opponent's best effort in 2015-16. Curry continued to score. And the Warriors continued to win. The all-time regular-season record was in sight.

Michael Jordan and the Chicago Bulls went 72-10 in 1995-96. Many thought that no team would ever break that record.

NBA Commissioner Adam Silver presents Curry with the MVP award in 2016.

FAST FACT

Golden State's head coach, Steve Kerr, once played for the Bulls. He was on their championship team that held the wins record for exactly 20 years.

Curry and the Warriors had four games left in the season. They needed to win all of them to get 73 wins—and the record. Two of those were against the San Antonio Spurs, who went on to win 67 games. But Golden State won both, and a third against the Memphis Grizzlies, to set up a chance for history back in Oakland.

Curry scored 46 points in the season finale. He made 10 three-pointers as the Warriors dominated the Grizzlies 125-104. Warriors fans rocked Oracle Arena in celebration of the 73-9 record.

Warriors fans packed Oracle Arena to see Curry and the Warriors go for a record 73rd win.

Curry drives to the hoop in the second half of the Warriors' record-setting win over Memphis.

Curry is a fan favorite at Oracle Arena and with Warriors fans everywhere.

Curry got hurt in the playoffs. He missed six games with ankle and knee injuries over the first two series. Still, the Warriors kept winning. They made it back to the NBA Finals and were one victory short of repeating as champions.

This time LeBron James and the Cavaliers prevailed. They won the last three games of the series, and Curry and the Warriors were defeated. Their future, though, remained bright. Curry vowed to keep the memory of the loss fresh in his mind. It motivated him and the Warriors to stay together and chase another title.

FAST FACT

The Warriors were the 10th team in history to overcome a 3-1 series deficit in the playoffs. They beat Oklahoma City in three straight games to take the Western Conference Finals.

TIMELINE

1988
Stephen Curry is born in Akron, Ohio, on March 14.

2006
Curry scores 15 points with 13 turnovers in his first college game.

2008
Led by Curry's 33 points, Davidson College upsets Wisconsin in the NCAA tournament.

2009
The Golden State Warriors take Curry seventh overall in the NBA Draft.

2013
Curry scores a career-high 54 points at New York on February 27.

2013
Curry plays in his first NBA playoff game at Denver on April 20.

2015
Curry and the Warriors beat Cleveland to win the NBA Finals.

2016
Curry breaks his own NBA single-season record for three-pointers made.

2016
Curry wins his second MVP award on May 10.

GLOSSARY

ASSIST
A pass that leads directly to a scored basket.

OVERTIME
An extra period or periods played in the event of a tie.

REBOUND
Grabbing a missed shot in basketball.

ROOKIE
A first-year player.

SCHOLARSHIP
Money given to a student to pay for education expenses.

SOPHOMORE
A student's second year in school.

STEAL
When a player takes the ball from the other team.

SWEEP
Winning every game in a series.

SWISH
When a made shot only touches the net and not the rim.

INDEX

ABOUT THE AUTHOR

Dave Campbell has been a sports writer for the Associated Press since 2000. He lives with his wife and son in Minneapolis.